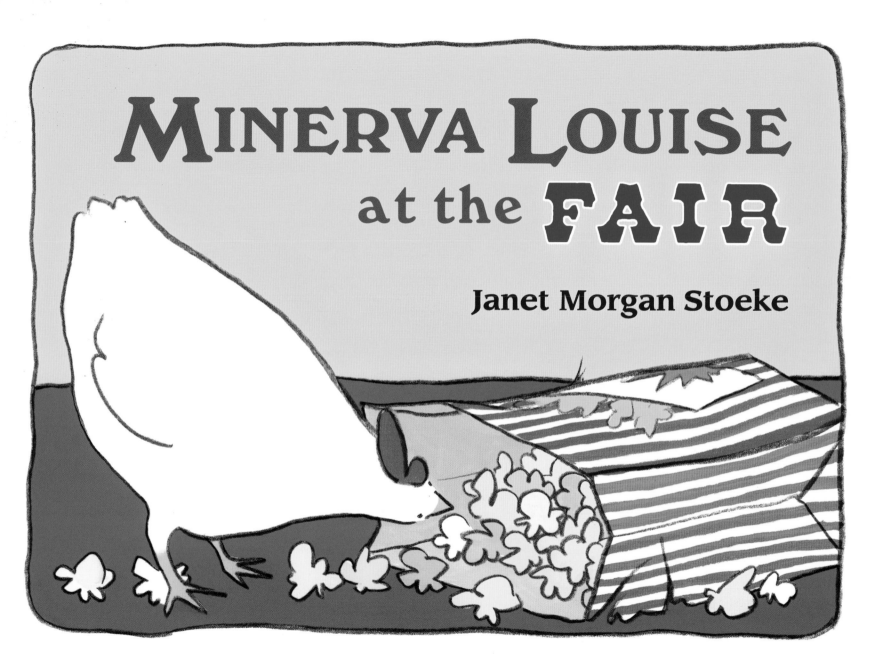

MINERVA LOUISE
at the FAIR

Janet Morgan Stoeke

DUTTON CHILDREN'S BOOKS • NEW YORK

Copyright © 2000 by Janet Morgan Stoeke
All rights reserved.

CIP Data is available.

Published in the United States 2000 by Dutton Children's Books,
a division of Penguin Putnam Books for Young Readers
345 Hudson Street, New York, New York 10014
www.penguinputnam.com
First Edition   Printed in Hong Kong
1 3 5 7 9 10 8 6 4 2
ISBN 0-525-46439-5

For my father,
J. PAUL STOEKE

Minerva Louise loved how
peaceful the farm was at night.

She stared up at the stars and listened to the
crickets long after everyone else was asleep.

BOOM! That's not a cricket. BOOM!

What is it? BOOM! I'd better go see what's happening.

Look at that! The stars are coming down from the sky!

And they're landing everywhere—on top of the mountains and all over the houses!

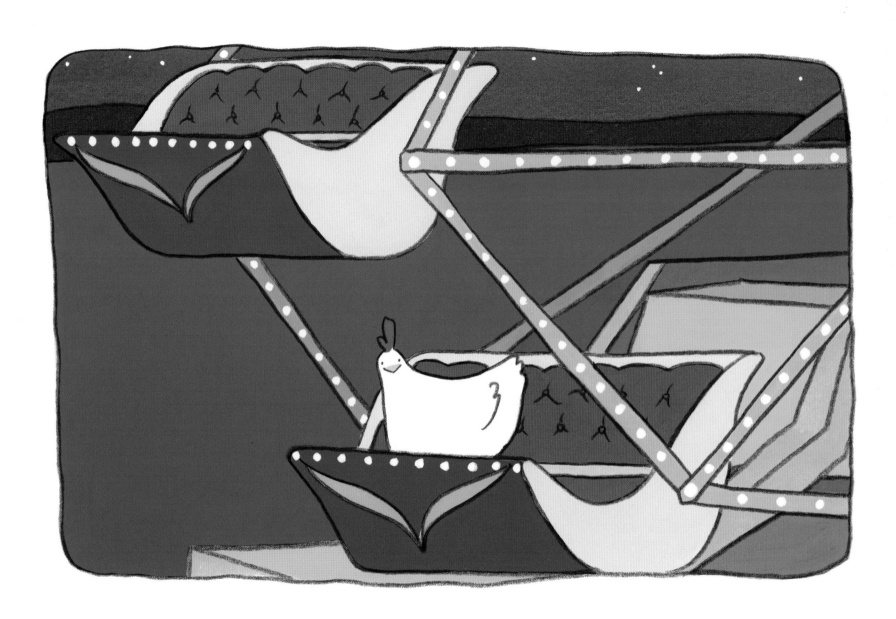

Even this bulldozer has stars on it.

Oooh! And it goes way up high.
Hey, I think I see some hens down there.

Oh, no. Those are just some stuffy old roosters.
They're no fun to play with.

Here are lots of nice hens!
But I can't get inside to play with them.

Hmm. And these hens are all sleeping. Maybe I should rest, too. I'm getting pretty tired.

I just need to find the henhouse.

I do hope it's as pretty as the horse barn!

When she finally found the henhouse,
Minerva Louise could hardly keep her eyes open.

She found one empty nest,
so she climbed in and went to sleep.

In the morning, she woke up
to a whole flock of farmers.

One of them was her farmer.
He got all excited when he saw her.

He even gave her a ride home in the truck.

And when they got back to the barn, he made

Minerva Louise a wonderful new nesting box....

…with some stars of her very own.